Another Little Book of
Farmya~~rd~~ ~~Tales~~

Heather Amery
Illustrated by Stephen Cartwright

Edited by Jenny Tyler
Language Consultant: Betty Root

Cover design by Hannah Ahmed

There is a little yellow duck to find on every page.

SURPRISE
VISITORS

This is Apple Tree Farm.

This is Mrs. Boot, the farmer. She has two children, called Poppy and Sam, and a dog called Rusty.

Today is Saturday.

Mrs. Boot, Poppy and Sam are having breakfast.
"Why are the cows so noisy?" asks Sam.

They all run out to the field.

The cows are running around the field. They are scared. A big balloon is floating over the trees.

"It's a hot air balloon."

"It's coming down," says Mrs. Boot. "It's going to land in our field." The balloon hits the ground.

There are two people in it.

"Where are we?" asks the man. "This is Apple Tree Farm. You frightened our cows," says Mrs. Boot.

The man climbs out.

"I'm Alice and this is Tim," says the woman.
"We ran out of gas. Sorry about your cows."

"A truck is following us."

"There it is now," says Alice. "Our friend is bringing more cylinders of gas for the balloon."

Alice helps to unload the truck.

Tim unloads the empty cylinders. Then he puts the new ones into the balloon's basket.

They blow up the balloon.

Poppy and Sam help Tim hold open the balloon.
A fan blows hot air into it. It gets bigger and bigger.

"Would you like a ride?"

"Oh, yes please," says Poppy. "Just a little one," says Tim. "The truck will bring you back."

Mrs. Boot, Poppy and Sam climb in.

Tim lights the gas burner. The big flames make a loud noise. "Hold on tight," says Alice.

The balloon goes up.

Slowly it leaves the ground. Tim turns off the burner. "The wind is blowing us along," he says.

The balloon floats along.

"I can see our farm down there," says Poppy.
"Look, there's Alice in the truck," says Sam.

"We're going down now," says Tim.

The balloon floats down and the basket lands in a field. Mrs. Boot helps Poppy and Sam out.

"Thank you very much."

They wave as the balloon takes off again.
"We were flying," says Sam.

16

MARKET
DAY

This is Apple Tree Farm.

This is Mrs. Boot, the farmer. She has two children, called Poppy and Sam, and a dog called Rusty.

Today is market day.

Mrs. Boot puts the trailer on the car.
Poppy and Sam put a wire crate in the trailer.

They drive to the market.

Mrs. Boot, Poppy and Sam walk past cows, sheep and pigs. They go to the shed which has cages of birds.

There are different kinds of geese.

"Let's look in all the cages," says Mrs. Boot.
"I want four nice young geese."

"There are four nice white ones."

"They look nice and friendly," says Poppy.
"Yes, they are just what I want," says Mrs. Boot.

A woman is selling the geese.

"How much are the four white ones?" asks Mrs. Boot. "I'll buy them, please." She pays for them.

"We'll come back later."

"Let's look at the other birds," says Sam. There are cages with hens, chicks, ducks and pigeons.

"Look at the poor little duck."

"It's lonely," says Poppy. "Please may I buy it?
I can pay for it with my own money."

"Yes, you can buy it."

"We'll get it when we come back for the geese,"
says Mrs. Boot. Poppy pays the man for the duck.

Mrs. Boot brings the crate.

Poppy opens the lid. The woman passes the geese to Mrs. Boot. She puts them in the crate.

One of the geese runs away.

A goose jumps out of the crate just before Sam shuts the door. It runs very fast out of the shed.

"Catch that goose."

Mrs. Boot, Poppy and Sam run after the goose.
The goose jumps through an open car door.

"Now we've got it," says Sam.

But a woman opens a door on the other side.
The goose jumps out of the car and runs away.

"Run after it," says Mrs. Boot.

The goose runs into the plant tent.
"There it is," says Sam, and picks it up.

"Let's go home," says Mrs. Boot.

"I've got my geese now." "And I've got my duck," says Poppy. "Markets are fun," says Sam.

THE SNOW STORM

This is Apple Tree Farm.

This is Mrs. Boot, the farmer. She has two children, called Poppy and Sam, and a dog called Rusty.

In the night there was a big snow storm.

In the morning, it is still snowing. "You must wrap up warm," says Mrs. Boot to Poppy and Sam.

Ted works on the farm.

He helps Mrs. Boot look after the animals.
He gives them food and water every day.

"Come and help me," calls Ted.

"Where are you going?" says Poppy.
"I'm taking this hay to the sheep," says Ted.

Poppy and Sam pull the hay.

They go out of the farmyard with Ted.
They walk to the gate of the sheep field.

"Where are the sheep?" says Sam.

"They are all covered with snow," says Ted.
"We'll have to find them," says Poppy.

They brush the snow off the sheep.

Ted, Poppy and Sam give each sheep lots of hay.
"They've got nice warm coats," says Sam.

Poppy counts the sheep.

"There are only six sheep. One is missing," says Poppy. "It's that naughty Woolly," says Ted.

They look for Woolly.

They walk around the snowy field.
"Rusty, good dog, find Woolly," calls Sam.

Rusty runs across the field.

Ted, Poppy and Sam run after him. Rusty
barks at the thick hedge.

Ted looks under the hedge.

"Can you see anything?" says Sam. "Yes, Woolly is hiding in there. Clever Rusty," says Ted.

"Come on, Woolly."

"Let me help you out, old girl," says Ted.
Carefully he pulls Woolly out of the hedge.

"There's something else!"

"Look, I can see something moving," says Sam.
"What is it, Ted?" says Poppy.

Ted lifts out a tiny lamb.

"Woolly has had a lamb," he says. "We'll take it and Woolly to the barn. They'll be warm there."

Poppy rides home.

She holds the lamb. "What a surprise!"
she says. "Good old Woolly."

THE GRUMPY GOAT

This is Apple Tree Farm.

This is Mrs. Boot, the farmer. She has two children, called Poppy and Sam, and a dog called Rusty.

Ted works on the farm.

He tells Poppy and Sam to clean the goat's shed.
"Will she let us?" asks Sam. "She's so grumpy now."

Gertie the goat chases Sam.

She butts him with her head. He nearly falls over.
Sam, Poppy and Rusty run out through the gate.

Poppy shuts the gate.

They must get Gertie out of her pen so they can get to her shed. "I have an idea," says Sam.

Sam gets a bag of bread.

"Come on, Gertie," says Sam. "Nice bread."
Gertie eats it and the bag, but stays in her pen.

"Let's try some fresh grass," says Poppy.

Poppy pulls up some grass and drops it by the gate. Gertie eats it but trots back into her pen.

"I have another idea," says Sam.

"Gertie doesn't butt Ted. She wouldn't butt me if I looked like Ted," says Sam. He runs off again.

Sam comes back wearing Ted's clothes.

He has found Ted's old coat and hat. Sam goes into the pen but Gertie still butts him.

"I'll get a rope," says Poppy.

They go into the pen. Poppy tries to throw the rope over Gertie's head. She misses.

Gertie chases them all.

Rusty runs out of the pen and Gertie follows him.
"She's out!" shouts Sam. "Quick, shut the gate."

Sam and Poppy clean out Gertie's shed.

They sweep up the old straw and put it in the wheelbarrow. They spread out fresh straw.

Poppy opens the gate.

"Come on, Gertie. You can go back now," says
Sam. Gertie trots back into her pen.

"You are a grumpy old goat," says Poppy.

"We've cleaned out your shed and you're still grumpy," says Sam. "Grumpy Gertie."

Next morning, they meet Ted.

"Come and look at Gertie now," says Ted. They all go to the goat pen.

Gertie has a little kid.

"Oh, isn't it sweet," says Poppy. "Gertie doesn't look grumpy now," says Sam.

CAMPING
OUT

This is Apple Tree Farm.

This is Mrs. Boot, the farmer. She has two children, called Poppy and Sam, and a dog called Rusty.

A car stops at the gate.

A man, a woman and a boy get out. "Hello," says the man. "May we camp on your farm?"

"Yes, you can camp over there."

"We'll show you the way," says Mr. Boot.
The campers follow in their car.

The campers put up their tent.

Poppy and Sam help them. They take chairs,
a table, a cooking stove and food out of the car.

Then they all go to the farmhouse.

Mrs. Boot gives the campers a bucket of water and some milk. Poppy and Sam bring some eggs.

"Can we go camping?"

"Please Dad, can we put up our tent too?"
says Poppy. "Oh yes, please Dad," says Sam.

Mr. Boot gets out the tent.

Poppy and Sam try to put up the little blue tent
but it keeps falling down. At last it is ready.

"Come and have supper."

"Then you can go to the tent," says Mrs. Boot.
"But you must wash and brush your teeth first."

73

Poppy and Sam go to the tent.

"It's not dark yet," says Sam. "Come on, Rusty.
You can come camping with us," says Poppy.

Poppy and Sam go to bed.

They crawl into the tent and tie up the door.
Then they wriggle into their sleeping bags.

"What's that noise?"

Sam sits up. "There's something walking around outside the tent," says Sam. "What is it?"

Poppy looks out of the tent.

"It's only old Daisy, the cow," she says. "She must have strayed into this field. She's so nosy."

Daisy looks into the tent.

Rusty barks at her. Daisy is scared. She tries to back away but the tent catches on her head.

Daisy pulls at the tent.

She pulls it down and runs off with it. Rusty chases her. Poppy and Sam run back to the house.

Mr. Boot opens the door.

"Hello, Dad," says Sam. "Daisy's got our tent."
"I think camping is fun," says Poppy.

THE NEW PONY

This is Apple Tree Farm.

This is Mrs. Boot, the farmer. She has two children, called Poppy and Sam, and a dog called Rusty.

Mr. Boot, Poppy and Sam go for a walk.

They see a new pony. "She belongs to Mr. Stone, who's just bought Old Gate Farm," says Mr. Boot.

The pony looks sad.

Her coat is rough and dirty. She looks hungry.
It looks as though no one takes care of her.

Poppy tries to stroke the pony.

"She's not very friendly," says Sam. "Mr. Stone says she's bad tempered," says Mr. Boot.

Poppy feeds the pony.

Every day, Poppy takes her apples and carrots.
But she always stays on the other side of the gate.

One day, Poppy takes Sam with her.

They cannot see the pony anywhere. The field looks empty. "Where is she?" says Sam.

Poppy and Sam open the gate.

Rusty runs into the field. Poppy and Sam are a bit
scared. "We must find the pony," says Poppy.

"There she is," says Sam.

The pony has caught her head collar in the fence.
She has been eating the grass on the other side.

Poppy and Sam run home to Mr. Boot.

"Please come and help us, Dad," says Poppy. "The pony is caught in the fence. She will hurt herself."

Mr. Boot walks up to the pony.

He unhooks the pony's head collar from the fence.
"She's not hurt," says Mr. Boot.

"The pony's chasing us."

"Quick, run," says Sam. "It's all right," says Poppy, patting the pony. "She just wants to be friends."

They see an angry man. It is Mr. Stone.

"Leave my pony alone," says Mr. Stone. "And get out of my field." He waves his stick at Poppy.

The pony is afraid of Mr. Stone.

Mr. Stone tries to hit the pony with his stick. "I'm going to get rid of that nasty animal," he says.

Poppy grabs his arm.

"You mustn't hit the pony," she cries. "Come on Poppy," says Mr. Boot. "Let's go home."

Next day, there's a surprise for Poppy.

The pony is at Apple Tree Farm. "We've bought her for you," says Mrs. Boot. "Thank you," says Poppy.

THE OLD
STEAM TRAIN

This is Apple Tree Farm.

This is Mrs. Boot, the farmer. She has two children, called Poppy and Sam, and a dog called Rusty.

"Hurry up," says Mrs. Boot.

"Where are we going today?" asks Poppy.
"To the old station," says Mrs. Boot.

They walk down the lane.

"Why are we going? There aren't any trains," says Sam. "Just you wait and see," says Mrs. Boot.

"What's everyone doing?" asks Poppy.

"They're cleaning up the old station," says
Mrs. Boot. "Everyone's helping today."

"There's lots to do."

"Poppy and Sam can help me," says the painter.
"Coats off and down to work," says Mrs. Boot.

Poppy and Sam work hard.

Sam brings pots of paint and Poppy brings the brushes. Mrs. Boot sweeps the platform.

"What's that noise?"

"It's the train. It's coming," says Mrs. Boot. "Look, it's a steam train," says Poppy. "How exciting."

The train puffs down the track.

It stops at the platform. The engine gives a long whistle. Everyone cheers and waves.

"Look, there's Dad," says Sam.

"He's helping the train driver, just for today," says Mrs. Boot. "Isn't he lucky?" says Poppy.

"All aboard," says Mrs. Boot.

"I'll get on here," says Poppy. "Come on, Rusty," says Sam. "I'll shut the door," says Mrs. Boot.

"Where are you going?"

"Aren't you coming with us?" asks Sam. "You stay on the train," says Mrs. Boot. "I'll be back soon."

"Look, there she is."

"She's wearing a cap," says Poppy. "Yes, I'm the guard, just for today," says Mrs. Boot.

Mrs. Boot waves a flag.

The train whistles and starts to puff away. Mrs. Boot jumps on the train and shuts the door.

"We're off," says Sam.

The train chugs slowly down the track. "Doesn't the old station look good now?" says Poppy.

"I like steam trains," says Sam.

"The station is open again," says Mrs. Boot. "And we can ride on the steam train every weekend."

DOLLY AND
THE TRAIN

This is Apple Tree Farm.

This is Mrs. Boot, the farmer. She has two children called Poppy and Sam, and a dog called Rusty.

Today there is a school outing.

Mrs. Boot, Poppy and Sam walk down the road to
the old station. "Come on, Rusty," says Sam.

"There's your teacher," says Mrs. Boot.

"And there's the old steam train, all ready for our outing," says Poppy.

"All aboard," says the driver.

The children and their teacher climb on the train.
The guard closes the door and blows his whistle.

Mrs. Boot waves goodbye.

The train puffs slowly down the track. Rusty barks at it. He wants to go on the outing too.

The children look out of the window.

"I can see Farmer Dray's farm," says Sam. "Why has the train stopped?" asks Poppy.

"The engine has broken down."

"We'll have to send for help," says the driver. "It won't be long." The guard runs across the fields.

"Here's a ladder."

"You can all get off now," says the driver. "We can have our picnic here," says the teacher.

"Let's go into the field," says Sam.

The children climb over the fence. "Stop! Come back, children," says the teacher. "There's a bull."

"It's only Buttercup."

"She's not a bull. She's a very nice cow," says
Poppy. "Well, come back here," says the teacher.

"Look, there's Farmer Dray."

"He's brought Dolly with him," says Sam. "A horse is no good. We need an engine," says the teacher.

The children watch.

Farmer Dray has a long rope. He leads Dolly along the train. The driver unhitches the engine.

The children climb back on the train.

"We'll soon be off now," says the teacher. "Dolly's ready," says Farmer Dray.

"Pull away, Dolly."

Dolly pulls and pulls. Very slowly the train starts to move. Farmer Dray walks along with Dolly.

They reach the station.

"Out by engine, back by horse," says Farmer Dray.
"That was a good outing," says Sam.

RUSTY'S
TRAIN RIDE

This is Apple Tree Farm.

This is Mrs. Boot, the farmer. She has two children, called Poppy and Sam, and a dog called Rusty.

They are having breakfast.

"What are we doing today?" says Sam. "Let's go and see the old steam train," says Mrs. Boot.

"Come on, Rusty," says Sam.

They walk down the road to the station. "Don't let Rusty go. Hold him tight," says Mrs. Boot.

They wait on the platform.

Mrs. Boot, Poppy and Sam watch the train come in.
Mrs. Hill and her puppy watch with them.

The train is ready to go.

Everyone talks to the train driver. The fireman shuts the doors. He climbs on the train.

"Where's my puppy?"

"Mopp was with me on the platform," says Mrs. Hill. "Now he's gone." The train starts to move.

Rusty watches it go.

He pulls and pulls and runs away. Then he jumps through an open carriage window.

"Come back, Rusty," shouts Sam.

Rusty looks out of the window. "There he is," says
Poppy. "He's going for a train ride on his own."

"Stop, stop the train," shouts Sam.

Mrs. Boot, Poppy and Sam shout and wave.
But the train puffs away down the track.

"What shall we do?"

"Both dogs have gone," says Sam. "We'll have to wait for the train to come back," says Mrs. Boot.

At last, the train comes back.

"Look, there's Rusty," says Sam. "You naughty dog, where have you been?" says Poppy.

The train stops at the station.

The fireman climbs down from the engine.
He opens the carriage door.

"Come on, Rusty."

"Your ride on the train is over," says Mrs. Boot.
Rusty jumps down. "What's he got?" says Sam.

"It's my little Mopp."

Mrs. Hill picks up her puppy. "Poor little thing.
Did you go on the train all by yourself?"

"Rusty went with him," says Sam.

"That's why he jumped on the train," says Poppy.
"Clever Rusty," says Sam.

WOOLLY STOPS
THE TRAIN

This is Apple Tree Farm.

This is Mrs. Boot, the farmer. She has two children called Poppy and Sam, and a dog called Rusty.

This is Ted.

He drives the tractor and helps Mrs. Boot on the farm. He waves and shouts to Mrs. Boot.

"What's the matter, Ted?" asks Mrs. Boot.

"The train is in trouble. I think it's stuck. I can hear it whistling and whistling," says Ted.

"We'll go and look."

"Poppy and Sam can come too," says Mrs. Boot.
"And Rusty," says Sam. They walk across the fields.

Soon they come to the train track.

They can just see the old steam train. It has stopped but is still puffing and whistling.

"Look at those sheep."

"They are on the track," says Poppy. "That's why the train has stopped." "Silly sheep," says Sam.

"It's that naughty Woolly."

"She's escaped from her field again," says Poppy.
"She wanted to see the steam train," says Sam.

"We must move them."

"You can help me," says Mrs. Boot. "Come on, Rusty," says Sam. They walk up to the sheep.

"How can we get them home?"

"We can't get them up the bank," says Ted.
"We'll put them on the train," says Mrs. Boot.

"Come on, Woolly."

They drive the sheep down the track to the train.
Woolly runs away but Rusty chases her back.

155

"We'll lift them up."

"Please help me, Ted," says Mrs. Boot. Ted and Mrs. Boot lift the sheep up into the carriage.

"All aboard!"

Poppy, Sam, Mrs. Boot, Ted and Rusty climb up into the carriage. Mrs. Boot waves to the driver.

The train puffs along.

It stops at the station. Mrs. Boot opens the door.
Poppy and Sam jump down onto the platform.

"How many passengers?" says the guard.

"Six sheep, one dog and four people," says Mrs. Boot. "That's all."

"Let's all go home now," says Mrs. Boot.

They take the sheep back to the farm. "I think Woolly just wanted a ride on the train," says Sam.

This edition first published in 2003 by Usborne Publishing Ltd., Usborne House, 83-85 Saffron Hill, London EC1N 8RT, England.
www.usborne.com